The Gingerbread Bear

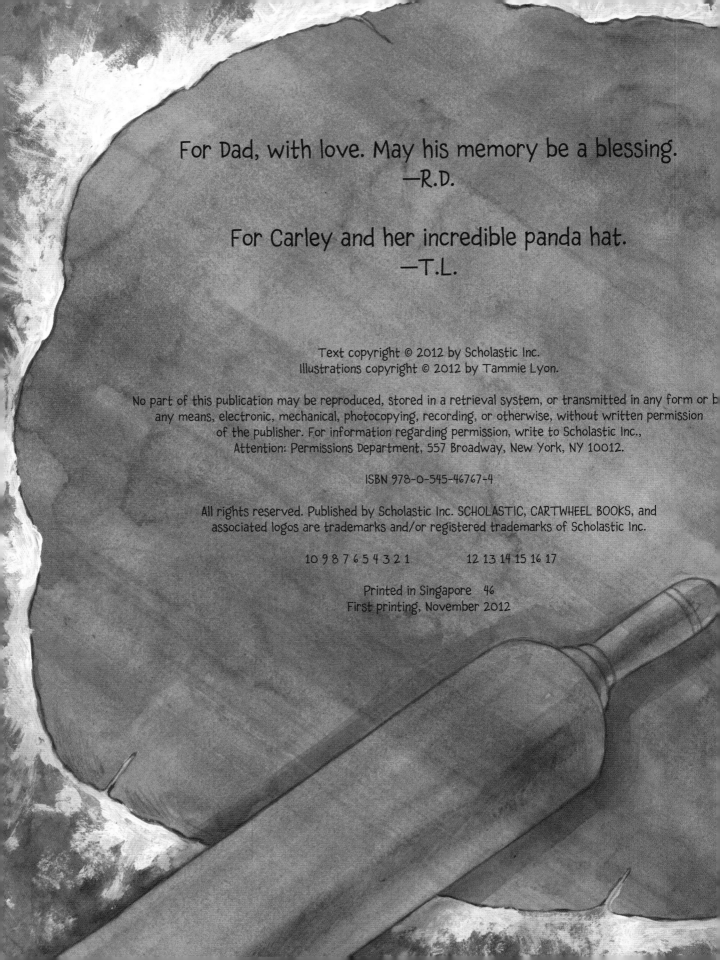

For Dad, with love. May his memory be a blessing.
—R.D.

For Carley and her incredible panda hat.
—T.L.

10 9 8 7 6 5 4 3 2 1   12 13 14 15 16 17

Printed in Singapore   46
First printing, November 2012

The Gingerbread Bear

By
Robert Dennis

Illustrated by
Tammie Lyon

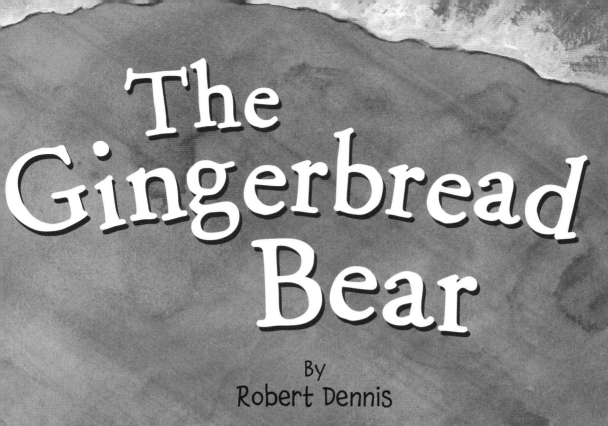

Cartwheel Books
An imprint of Scholastic Inc.

Once upon a time,
there was a clever park ranger
and a sweet mom and a little girl
who lived in Woodlands National Park.

One day the sweet mom said to the little girl,
"I will make a cookie just for you."
"Can it be a Gingerbread Bear?" asked the little girl.

The sweet mom put the
Gingerbread Bear into the pan.
And she put the pan into the oven.

"Now listen for the timer," said the sweet mom.
"And when the buzzer rings, call me.
But do not open the door."

Then the clever ranger kissed
his wife and daughter and left for work.
The sweet mom went out to the garden.

The little girl sat in the kitchen and watched the oven.
Soon she could smell the Gingerbread Bear.

"I want to see if the Gingerbread Bear
has finished hibernating,"
said the little girl just as the timer went off.

As she started to pull back the oven door,
paws pushed it wide open.

The Gingerbread Bear
jumped out of the pan.
He jumped out of the oven.

The Gingerbread Bear ran across the kitchen to the open door. The little girl ran to shut the door, but the Gingerbread Bear ran faster.

He ran out the door and down the steps and onto the road in Woodlands National Park.

Then he roared,
"Run, run, try if you dare.
You can't catch me.
I'm the Gingerbread Bear!"

The little girl ran after him.

The sweet mom saw the Gingerbread Bear. And she ran, too. But the Gingerbread Bear ran faster. And the little girl and the sweet mom had to sit down and rest.

The Gingerbread Bear kept running.
Soon he came to three campers.

"Where are you going?"
shouted the campers.

"I have run away from
a little girl and a sweet mom.
And I can run away from you, too,"
said the Gingerbread Bear.

"Oh, you can, can you?" said the campers.
And the campers ran after him.

Then the Gingerbread Bear growled,
"Run, run, try if you dare.
You can't catch me.
I'm the Gingerbread Bear!"

The campers ran fast.
But the Gingerbread Bear ran faster.

And the campers had to sit down to rest.

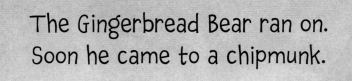

The Gingerbread Bear ran on.
Soon he came to a chipmunk.

"Where are you going?" asked the chipmunk.

"I have run away from
a little girl and a sweet mom
and three campers.
And I can run away from you, too,"
said the Gingerbread Bear.

"Oh, you can, can you?" the chipmunk said.
And he began to run after the Gingerbread Bear.

Then the Gingerbread Bear called out,
"Run, run try if you dare.
You can't catch me.
I'm the Gingerbread Bear!"

The chipmunk ran fast.
But the Gingerbread Bear ran faster.

And the chipmunk had to sit down to rest.

The Gingerbread Bear ran on.
Soon he came to a gray wolf.

"Where are you going?" asked the wolf.

"I have run away from
a little girl and a sweet mom
and three campers and a chipmunk.
And I can run away from you, too,"
said the Gingerbread Bear.

"Oh, you can, can you?" said the wolf.
And he began to run after the Gingerbread Bear.

Then the Gingerbread Bear screamed out,
"Run, run, try if you dare.
You can't catch me.
I'm the Gingerbread Bear!"

The wolf ran fast.
But the Gingerbread Bear ran faster.

And the wolf had to sit down to rest.

The Gingerbread Bear ran on.
Soon he smelled honey and approached a house.

He went inside. The Gingerbread Bear looked at the table.

There sat a clever ranger

and a sweet mom

and a chipmunk

and a little girl

and three campers

and a wolf.

He ran around the table and said,
"Run, run, try if you dare.
You can't catch me.
I'm the Gingerbread Bear."

The clever ranger said,
"I can't hear you, Gingerbread Bear.
Come a little closer."

The Gingerbread Bear stopped running.
He came a little closer to the clever ranger.

"I have run away from
a little girl and a sweet mom
and three campers
and a chipmunk and a wolf.

And I can run away from you, too,"
said the Gingerbread Bear.

"I still can't hear you," said the clever ranger.
"Come a little closer."

The Gingerbread Bear came
very close to the clever ranger.

"Oh, you can, can you?"
said the clever ranger.

And snip-snap!
That was the end of that!